Joseph Pennell

The Jew at Home

Impressions of a Summer and Autumn Spent with Him

Joseph Pennell

The Jew at Home
Impressions of a Summer and Autumn Spent with Him

ISBN/EAN: 9783337376659

Printed in Europe, USA, Canada, Australia, Japan

Cover: Foto ©Andreas Hilbeck / pixelio.de

More available books at **www.hansebooks.com**

THE JEW AT HOME

IMPRESSIONS OF A SUMMER AND AUTUMN
SPENT WITH HIM

BY

JOSEPH PENNELL

WITH ILLUSTRATIONS BY THE AUTHOR

NEW YORK
D. APPLETON AND COMPANY
1892

PREFACE.

A LARGE portion of the following sketches appeared in the *Illustrated London News* during the month of December, 1891. But their reappearance now gives me an opportunity of making a few explanations and stating a few facts.

I went to southeastern Europe last summer with no thought of the Jew or his affairs in my head. I had no idea that almost daily for five months I should see him under all conditions of life—in fact, that I should be unable to escape from him. I may have formed certain conclusions about him, but I have not stated them, and do not intend to. I have been

told repeatedly by Jews and Christians, who
either have never seen the Jew at home or else
have spent a few weeks with him under the
most favorable circumstances, that I had no
right to discuss the matter, since I had not
studied the subject in all its bearings ever since
the first appearance of the Jew on the face of
the earth. I have, however, had the opportunity thrust upon me of seeing the Jew much
more intimately than the majority of his defenders or his detractors; and what I did see
I have simply put down in black and white.
It requires no knowledge of life five hundred
years ago to see how the Polish Jew is living
to-day. What may have made the Austro-Hungarian or Russian Jew the most contemptible
specimen of humanity in Europe it is not my
purpose to discuss. What makes him dreaded
by the peasant, what makes him hated by the
proprietor, what makes him loathed by people
of every religion, and what makes him despised
by his fellow-religionists of the better class who

live with him and know him I have no intention of entering deeply into. If any one does
not believe these things, let him go to southeastern Europe and he will find them out
quickly enough. He must look for himself,
however, and not rely upon people who are
only too ready to prevent him from seeing anything of the real state of affairs.

I am neither a Jew hater nor a Jew lover.
I can sympathize with the oppressed Jews of
Russia, and also with the Hungarians who are
thoroughly sick of those they already have, and
who are doing all they can to keep from im-
porting any more. And here I should like to
bring forward some rather curious facts which
have been very cleverly ignored. The Russians
who have got the Jews in their own territory
are going to get rid of them. The Turks have
made laws refusing to receive them. And Germany and Austria-Hungary are loudly calling
upon the rest of the world to take up collec-
tions to prevent their settling in either empire.

Is it not rather singular that the Jews of Hamburg, of Vienna, of Buda-Pesth, who are stirring up the world with the stories of Russian atrocities, should be so very careful that these oppressed people of the same race and the same religion should be sent away as far as possible from their own countries? One might think that these poor hounded wretches could be settled quite as comfortably in some corners of Germany or Austria-Hungary, where their language would be understood and where they would find friends, as away out in the unknown wilderness of South America. The most important part of the whole answer is perfectly simple. The minute the Jew gets out of Russia and into freedom he is ten times worse than while he was there—that is, so long as he is settled in a colony of his own people, or in large numbers in a Jew town. Here is my whole point. There is no doubt whatever that these Jews who have stood· persecution for centuries have in them many elements of good

which ought to be developed, which can be
developed, and which are developed almost
every time an individual Jew is given a chance.
The minute he learns that he has to stand or
fall by himself and for himself, that he has no
right to call himself a deserving subject of pity,
a down-trodden slave, an object of compassion
for shady millionaires and Dorcas meetings, he
does stand up and becomes a citizen of respecta-
bility and worth. But bring these miserable
Jews away or let them come away in colonies,
give them clothes and money and land and
plows and cattle, and help them in a way in
which you would never help any other men,
and they will ask for more, until they are strong
enough to drive everybody else out of that
part of the country in which they have settled.
If you do not believe this, go to the Austria-
Hungarian frontier and find out. Here they
have not been really helped; they were only
permitted to settle in large numbers, to enjoy
perfect freedom, and to preserve all their super-

stitious customs, their habits, and their costume, with the result that they intensified all those characteristics which in the end have made them so odious and have driven the Russians to get rid of them. Though the Austrian, as a civilized being, can not well throw these people out of his dominions, every Austrian citizen, Jew or Christian, is doing his best to prevent any more from coming into the country.

My last word is simply this: Treat the Jew, if he is brought to you, as an ordinary man; grant him no advantages which you would not give his Austrian, Polish, or German fellow-countryman, no matter what his religion is. Make him an Englishman or an American, break up his old customs, his clannishness, his dirt, and his filth—or he will break you.

Since writing the above, the articles which appeared in the *Illustrated London News* have been answered by a "Native of Brody," in the issue for January 9, 1892, page 55. Other newspapers have taken this matter up and chal-

lenged me to answer him. But the editor of
the *Illustrated London News*, from his stand-
point, thought he had published enough on the
subject, and did not see his way to printing
any more. I am therefore compelled to answer
the charges made against me here, not wishing
to go into a newspaper war. I challenged the
"Native of Brody" to allow me to include his
article in my book, but this you can hardly
expect one who can not distinguish the difference between Gentile and Christian to do. In
fact, the people who at the present time are
clamoring so wildly for the relief of the Russian Jew have not even as good arguments as
this "Native of Brody," and their only outlet
seems to be in contributing to *Darkest Russia* and appealing to hysterical persons whose
ignorance is only equaled by their grandilo-
quence.

While I have been told many flattering
things about my articles concerning The Jew
at Home by Jews themselves, it is even more

flattering to be taken so seriously by one who describes himself as "A Native of Brody."

Now, I do not doubt for a moment that this gentleman is a native of Brody, but the only charitable construction I can put upon his statements, by which he endeavors to refute what I saw with my own eyes, is that he has been so long away from the town that he has forgotten all about it, or that he only knew it in its more prosperous days. No doubt he can furnish portraits of Brody Jews who have no character at all. So could I, but I wanted to get the character of the place. Therefore I did draw "the particular type of Hebrew" who is the "average Jew of Brody," and if he is what my critic calls a Pharisee, he seems to have obeyed the law of his forefathers and increased and multiplied greatly. I repeat again that the majority of the people do nothing at all with their hands. And if the unbiased observer will go into the greater number of shops, enumerated by the "Native of Brody," he will see that to run them it is necessary only to be a salesman and a middleman. If he could also learn the comparative Jewish and Christian populations of the town, he would then be in a better condition to estimate how many Jews could be hewers of wood and drawers of water to the middle-class Christian. As the only person who by any stretch of imagination could be called a guide, from whom I obtained any information, was a Jew, it is rather curious that he should have furnished me with such false data, unless perhaps he wants himself to be helped out of the town of Brody.

My critic endeavors to compare Brody of thirty-five years ago with Brody of to-day, and then admits that no comparison is possible. It is only Brody of to-day which I described; and as the Jews are in such a large majority, why do they not make efforts to have their town better governed? He confuses Austria-Hungary and Brody so hopelessly that here it is rather difficult to follow his argument. If every im-

portant industry of Galicia owes its origin to
the Jews of Brody it is very much to their
credit. But of course I am speaking only of
Brody, where "factories and mills" are not
conspicuous features. It is to be regretted that
they have not concentrated some of their prac-
tical energy upon their own town. I do refer
to the Jewish hospitals. But in a town of the
size of Brody, where nearly all the people are
Jews, these are only what one would expect to
find. The charity of the Jews to their own people is a well-known fact.

In the next point which my critic seeks to
make against me he has unfortunately left out
one word. He says the sanitation in Brody is
as good as that of any other town in the Austria-
Hungarian monarchy (*sic*). He has forgotten
the qualification Jewish; had he said Jewish
town, I should have agreed with him. As it is,
his statement is as misleading as his strictures
on English towns are unjust. Doubtless those
portions of Whitechapel which are inhabited by

emigrants from Brody are as dirty as that town itself. I am glad to have his assurance of this fact. It but confirms my conclusion that when Polish Jews are settled in colonies in a new land they unfortunately bring old customs and habits along with them.

I have stated merely what I saw with my own eyes of the women of Brody, and I regret that I have nothing to retract in this respect. I am glad to know there is a Jewish theatre in Brody; I certainly did not see it. I also regret that, although I saw much of musical people in Buda-Pesth and other parts of Hungary, I never heard a word of the Musical Society of Brody, which my critic describes as one of the best in the country. As to my not having seen a religious ceremony in the synagogue, I endeavored to describe the conduct of the people during what I believe is called the Procession of the Sepharim. I took sufficient notice of the lamps and the brass plaques in the large synagogue to see that they must have been either of the

best old Dutch manufacture or beautiful copies
of them made by hand many years ago. As
for the many thousand more lamps, if they are
manufactured in Brody they are very careful
imitations of Brummagem machine-made goods,
and nothing like the beautiful old ones to which
I referred. I know that the clothes of the peasants were home-made once, and many of them
still are. But can the "Native of Brody" tell
me that the Jews do not preside over piles of
rubbish, which I suppose must be called clothes,
which they are trying to make the peasants exchange for their own beautiful home-made costume? that the handkerchiefs which all the
women wear on their heads are not the cheapest
printed stuffs? that cheap machine-made boots
are not taking the place of the old foot-coverings
that look more like moccasins? But why should
I go on through the list, merely to contradict a
man who does not agree with me, but who has
put forth no facts to prove me in the wrong, and
who finally has to fall back on personalities.

But I must add just one word more. My critic says I object to the Jew because he is clannish. I do, since when he comes or is brought even only so far away from Russia as to Brody, to Whitechapel, or to Vineland, New Jersey, he carries his customs, his habits, his race-prejudices—in fact, his clannishness—along with him. It is rather unfortunate, however, that my critic brought in the reference to Vineland, as the story of the complete collapse of this colony, and also of those established in South America, has made rather sad reading in the pages of the *Anti-Jacobin* for some weeks. I can recommend these articles to the "Native of Brody," and I hope with him that Baron Hirsch's scheme will not have the same ending.

3

CONTENTS.

LIST OF ILLUSTRATIONS.

THE JEW AT HOME.

I.

IN AUSTRIA AND HUNGARY.

THOUGH the Jew for some time past has been monopolizing the newspapers and public attention, my interest in him was never greatly aroused until this summer, when for myself I saw him as he really is in the southeast of Europe—as he is quite unknown in England or America. I met him first in Carlsbad, a miserable, weak, consumptive-looking specimen of humanity, a greasy corkscrew ringlet over each ear, head bent forward, coat-collar turned up, hands crossed on his stomach, each buried in the opposite sleeve, coat reaching to his heels, and a caricature of an umbrella under his arm. I had always supposed Carlsbad to be the favorite haunt of royalty, and now I found the most conspicuous people in the place were these creatures, so many pages out of German and Austrian comic papers. Then next I came across him in Vienna, in the Judengasse, still with the same curls, the same long coat, the same general greasiness and suggestion of physical incapacity. He was even more prominent in Buda-Pesth, where, in crowds, he haunted the old-clothes exchange in the yearly market, and where he seemed, if possible, a degree greasier and more degenerate. And now I began to hear a great deal about him — not only from the philanthropists who know him not, and therefore long to take him into their midst, but from those who, knowing him, long to get rid of him for evermore. In England, where one's sympathies are taxed in a fresh cause every day, one could read about "Philanthrope"

At Carlsbad for his health.

4

Hirsch and his Jews and remain indifferent; but it was impossible to stay in Austria or Hungary without feeling that the Jewish question

The Judengasse, Vienna.

was one of the most interesting problems of the day.

It is in these countries that one can best see him as he really is. In Russia persecution still lends him the dignity of the martyr; but in Austria and Hungary he is the free man, at

liberty to live as he chooses, to wear his ringlets, and to make his money by whatever means
suit him best—the free man he will be when
exported in hundreds from Russia and settled
in colonies in the new promised lands. Of the
progress he will make when left to his own
resources I had excellent opportunity to judge,
since I saw him in the Austro-Hungarian Empire, where he is the free citizen, as well as in
Russia, where he is the oppressed and down-
trodden victim. That he is cruelly treated by
the Russian Government is as certain as that
reports of this cruelty are grossly exaggerated.
One would as soon believe the Governor of
Kieff's assertion that no Jews had been expelled
from his city as many of the stories one hears
from the other side. In fact, one hardly knows
whether or not to accept the late announcement of the Russian authorities, that all repress-
ive measures against him have been stopped, or
the equally surprising statement made by his
friends, that he is still coming into Hamburg at

the rate of two or three thousand a day. But in all the stories and reports afloat about him small attention is paid to his present manner

In the market, Márámaros Sziget.

of life when he is free to regulate it for him- self, though this is a subject of far more im- mediate importance to the world than the his- tory of the cruelties and injustices that have developed or degraded him into what he is in

Russia. Nowhere could there be a better chance to study the emancipated Polish Jew than in Brody and Márámaros Sziget, the biggest Austrian and Hungarian Jewish cities; in Lemberg and in some of the smaller towns and villages of Galicia; and along the Russian frontier; and in all these places, in which few, if any, of his modern historians and defenders have been, I have seen him and considered him with that interest which he, there in such a powerful majority, commands. To write about his religion or his social and political condition is beyond my purpose; I merely wish to describe him as I saw him, to say something about how he lives and what he does.

Márámaros Sziget is a town of about sixteen thousand inhabitants, situated in the extreme northeastern part of Hungary. Among these sixteen thousand one can find almost all the races of that part of Europe, but considerably more than half the population to-day are Jews, and these are Polish and Russian Jews

who have come there within the last thirty or
forty years. It is a typical Hungarian town,
stretching out in almost every direction from
its large central square, its long streets inhabited mainly by Hungarians and Wallachs, who

In the Jews' quarter, Márámaros Sziget.

there build their one storied cottages and hide
themselves behind their high wooden fences.
When you get a glimpse into their yards, you
see the usual farmyard litter of any other coun-

try town. But unless the Jew has some business with these people, he is never in their quarter. To find him you must come down to the center of the town, where the great bulk of the eight or ten thousand Jews are herded together in one street, living no better than in Whitechapel. They have appropriated not only the old houses which lie at one end of the square, but half the large hotel and town buildings recently put up in the middle of it. And here they swarm, as if lodgings were as scarce and expensive as in the heart of a great city like London. They live in cellars and in garrets, in alley-ways and up courts, in a state of filth and dirt, which is brought out in stronger relief because of the comparative cleanliness of the peasant quarters.

With the exception of this filth—but this is horribly serious—there is little on the surface with which one can reproach them. They are always working, though rarely, if ever, with their hands; they are endlessly bargaining or

haggling about something. If a peasant brings
in a few watermelons, he turns them over to
the Jew middleman, who acts as commission

Jew with peasants to hire, Márámaros Sziget.

merchant—at what commission, however, I do
not know. If the peasant wants to be hired,
he usually goes not directly to the farmer, but
to the Jew, who at daybreak is arranging his
terms in the large central market-square and

5

in the court-yards surrounding it. In Márámaros Sziget, however, I saw Jews really doing something besides buying and selling; they
were the cab-drivers of the town. The only
other place where I found them making any
pretense to using their hands was in Berdicheff,
where a few were hiring themselves out as
wood-sawyers. In Kieff, those who were carters and cooks had been expelled.

If you ask the people of Márámaros Sziget
— whether the Hungarians or Germans, the
Ruthenians or Wallachs — about the Jew, not
one will have a good word to say for him. The
magistrate will tell you that there are more
Jews on his charge list than all the other people put together. This was a surprise to me,
because all through this part of the country,
where they abound, I found them quite as hon-
est and apparently as law-abiding as any one
else. They are hated by the bankers because
up here on the frontier, where there is much
money-changing to be done, their bank is in

their trousers' pockets and their office wherever
they can stop anybody who wants to do any
business. The peasant dislikes and yet fears
them, because in the bilingual or trilingual country they are the only persons among the lower
classes who take the trouble to learn three or
four languages. One hears in Máramaros Sziget,
and, indeed, in Transylvania, the same stories
of the Jew sweating the peasant and taking
his land which have been so often told in Russia, but for their truth I can not vouch; and,
in fact, I do not consider this Jewish trait of
much importance. If it is true, and the Jew
should try these little practices in England or
America, he would find that he had a very
different class of people to deal with.

One branch of trade which he has monopo-
lized hereabouts is inn-keeping, almost all the
inns, except the larger ones in the more important towns, being managed by Jews. Only
by a stretch of the imagination, however, can
the name "inn" be given to the usually lonely

house, with no bush or customary sign at the door, with a foul approach to it through the accumulation of refuse which has been thrown out and left there, and with, inside, a big, bare room, its furniture a few tables and the cage behind which the proprietor, as in all Hungarian inns, keeps his stock, or, not infrequently, nothing but a broken-down table, no less dilapidated chairs, and some framed Hebrew prints on the wall. Sometimes there is an inner room for more distinguished travelers, a Jew peddler, perhaps, or a well-to-do carter; but it is at the same time the family sleeping-room, where there is sure to be a squalling baby in a cradle and two or three friends of the proprietor talking over their affairs. I remember one day when a friend came in carrying, wrapped up in dirty paper, a lot of meat in a state in which I thought only a gypsy could have relished it, but which he displayed as a great bargain. You can only buy bread and wine in these places, or at times only bread and milk.

What one might get were one compelled to remain overnight, hermetically sealed up in this inner room, happily I am not prepared to say, any more than I am to explain why the Jew inn is the filthiest place imaginable, while the Hungarian inn, but a few miles off, in the same country, is often as clean as an English one.

While talking about this northeast corner of Hungary one might as well include Austrian Poland. The characteristics of Jewish life are quite the same in both; the only difference is in the size of the place where the Jews have settled. Podwoloczyska, a town of four or five hundred inhabitants, though only fifteen minutes from the frontier, is as fully developed a Jewish town as Entredam, about the same size, which is some twelve hours from the frontier in Transylvania. What I mean is that the minute the Jew is allowed to adopt the habits which the Christian finds so odious, he does so. But first he has to get out of Russia. Brody, the largest purely Jewish town in Austria-Hungary, is the most awful example of Jewish life I have ever seen. Once one of the free cities of the empire, and then a flourishing place, it

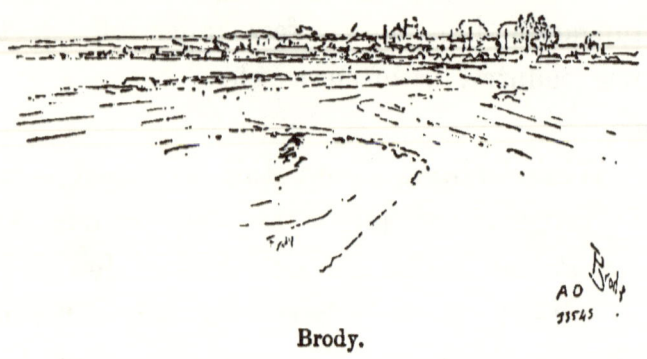

Brody.

became a center for Jews. It has now lost its freedom, but not its Jewish population. In the latter respect, indeed, it has rather gained. The town has become poorer and poorer, and so have its twenty thousand inhabitants. The friend of the Jew tells you that the Jew of Brody does not go away because he has not money enough; the Antisemite says he does not go because he does not want to. Any way, it

The market, Brody.

is quite evident that he stays there, while the commerce of the town has left it, that he seems perfectly content to loaf and idle all day, haggling in the public square, happy if he can gain enough money to pay for his supper. And it is this apparent idleness, this objection to manual work, which makes the Jew so hated, his coming so dreaded, all through Austria-Hungary, and more especially along the frontier. In a word, to sum up, the Austro-Hungarian Jew produces nothing, he lives on nothing, and apparently he wants nothing. His home is cheerless, his costume is disreputable, and he stands around doing nothing with his hands in a country where every one else of his class is at work, takes a pride in his home, and dresses like a picture.

6

II.

IN AUSTRIAN POLAND.

BRODY, the largest Jewish town in Austria-Hungary, lies so near the Russian frontier that that part of it which is not Jewish is almost Russian. Here, as at all the other frontier towns, three languages are spoken, but they are languages which are not studied by the average linguist — Polish, Russian, and Hebrew. Of course, every Jew, and this means almost everybody, talks a sort of German, while the chances are that the seediest may ask you where you come from in English, French, or Italian. For the Jew of this country is something like the Chinaman; he goes abroad to make a little money, and when he has made it, he comes home not to enjoy it, like the Italian, but to gain more, if he can, out of his fellow-country-men.

Brody is interesting, not only because it is the largest Jewish town in that part of Austria-Hungary which was formerly Poland, but because here one sees fully developed a curious architecture of which there are traces in Lemberg, Cracow, and Warsaw. The central part of the town is strongly built with great stone two-storied houses, which have huge iron doors on the ground floor and strong iron shutters to all the windows. These buildings were the store-houses of merchants when Brody was a prosperous commercial city; to-day they are the warrens in which burrow innumerable Jewish families. Late in the morning, for the Jew is not an early bird, they unbar the iron doors and come out; early in the evening they bar themselves up behind them for the night. Not even in the most important bank is there such a suggestion of strength about doors and windows, such an apparent fear that some one may break in. Naturally, people who bury themselves in warehouses never intended to be lived in can not expect to be overhealthy; and, to make matters worse, their refuse is all pitched into the street, which is nothing more than an open sewer. Their sanitary habits and customs are rather too primitive to be gone into.

In Brody and all the other towns I went to, save Lemberg (where there was a Jewish theatre, which I did not see, however, because it was closed), the Jews seemed to have no amusement except going to the synagogue. But I was in Brody during the celebration or anniversary of the Exodus, and at this they certainly were enjoying themselves. The chief synagogue in Brody is a huge square building, with a large hall for the men in the center, and on either side, like side aisles in a church, two smaller rooms for the women. Through narrow grated windows the latter look in on the ceremony, which that night seemed to have

Interior of the synagogue.

as great an attraction for them as it had for
me. The main hall was crowded with a pushing, struggling mass of men and boys. They
walked about, talked to friends in their loudest
tones, breaking off to chant responses or to
pray with that violent bending of the body
which, merely to look at, makes one almost
dizzy. Small boys ran up and down, carrying
little banners with lighted candles atop, or let
off squibs and fire-crackers. A lot of curious
ceremonies were gone through, the most singular of which, in one of the smaller synagogues,
was the unending dance of a number of men.
But what was most notable was that the place
was less like a church than a stock exchange
or a bourse, where every few minutes business
and talk were interrupted by the chanting of
responses and by prayers. It might have been
the synagogue denounced by Christ in Jerusalem nineteen hundred years ago. The squabbles
among the boys, always violently suppressed
by their elders; the ever-recurring striking of

the two great boards; the struggle to get up
on the central platform; the never-ending procession of the great scrolls, around and around;
the really beautiful singing which was heard at
times; the marvelous beauty of the old swing-
ing brass lamps in which this synagogue is so
rich; the haggling and the disputing—none of
these could let me forget for a minute the
awful stench of filthy human flesh which per-
vaded the place. I have been present at almost all the great religious festivals of Europe
in which people pack themselves together in
overheated and badly ventilated buildings for
hours, but never in my life, in any country or
under any conditions, have I been sickened by
such a smell as in these Jewish synagogues.
While the greater number of the men are in
the synagogue, many of the women devote themselves to their toilet, never taking the trouble
to close their curtainless windows. A walk
through the town at this hour will show one
a surprising series of realistic pictures of Susan-

The Jewish cemetery, Brody.

nah, and apparently the sight is so common
that it seems no longer to interest the elders.
Whether because the Jew delights in exhibit-
ing the interior of his house, or whether because of some old law which compelled him to
do everything in public, it is a fact that he per-
forms in a quite open manner all those functions usually considered strictly private. All
through this part of the country a window-cur-
tain in a Jew's house is almost unknown, and
privacy is unsought. On the other hand, there
is nothing to see in his house. Its interior is
the barest, most forlorn, most uninteresting
imaginable, and it is not, as far as I could discover, until after the Jew is dead that he has
the slightest pride in his looks. Then it seems
necessary that he should be buried with the
rest of his people under a tombstone some
eight or ten feet high, decorated in the most
fantastic fashion; one side is gilded elaborately, and covered with Hebrew characters, though
the other, perfectly plain, save for a tiny in-

scription, is unhewn and rough. But even here,
in their cemetery as in their quarter in the
town, the Jews are crowded and jostled to-

Going to the market.

gether. The graveyard of Brody, with the great
stones leading in every direction, backed up

A study of types, Brody.

against a deep, dark wood, through which, here
and there, you may see a long black figure
wandering, is one of the uncanniest places I
ever got into, and it had the same unkempt,
uncared-for look that is over every street and
square where the Jews live. However unwill-
ing or unable as the Jew is to spend money
on himself, he seems ready to spend it on his
neighbor. Miserable as is his own home, he
manages to support a large Jewish hospital,
which is reasonably clean and comfortable.

The weekly market was held while I was
in Brody. The peasants, who came from the
surrounding country, were all in more or less
picturesque costume, especially the women, but
the Jewesses of the town wore no distinctive
dress, though some of the better class had their
hair arranged in that horribly quaint fashion of
about 1850, and wore ear-rings of the same
awful period. There was no attempt, as in the
markets of so many Hungarian and Austrian
towns where Jews are few or none, to supply

the peasants with their own often beautiful costume. For, if in Europe there have been now
and then great Jewish musicians, great Jewish
poets and artists, it is no less true that the
average Jew all over the southeastern part of
the Continent is doing his best to crush out
all artistic sense in the peasants by supplant-
ing their really good handiwork with the vilest
machine-made trash that he can procure. He
himself is altogether without any appreciation
of beauty. In Brody, if one pointed to the
lovely old Dutch lamps in the synagogue as
proof to the contrary, the Jew would quickly
make it clear that his pride in them is really
due not to the loveliness of their design, but
to the price a *bric-à-brac* dealer from Vienna
once offered for them. The only things the
Jew had for sale in the Brody market were
old clothes, which may have come from Vienna
or Buda-Pesth, or anywhere else, apparently all
the old stove - pipe hats of Europe, and the
poorest, cheapest fabrics, which he was endeav-

He takes the greatest possible pride in his own costume.

oring to force the peasant to buy. It is a curious trait of the Polish Jew that, while he shows the keenest pride in his own ringlets, actually going to his barber to have them curled, shedding tears when, forced to serve his term in the Austrian army, they must be cut off; while he furls his dirty old caftan around him and proudly promenades about in his old *ceelynder*, which most people would consider worn out before he ever got it—in a word, while he takes the greatest possible pride in his costume, he takes the greatest possible pains to make all other people give up theirs. The Jew with clothes to sell is the same the world over. He rushes out and assails every one who passes in Brody, as in Whitechapel or New York. For a man whose sole aim in life is buying and selling, his methods are most unbusiness-like and repulsive.

The inquisitiveness of the Polish Jew is something one can not understand. There is an awful desire with him always to know where you came from and what you are doing. The minute this is gratified, however, he shows no further active interest in you, though he may have used half a dozen languages in trying to get the information. Once he has got it, he will simply stop and stand in front of you and stare, especially if you are, as I was, trying to draw the town. But when I questioned him about himself and his own affairs and prospects he had absolutely nothing to tell me. I started to make this drawing of the synagogue, but such a big crowd came and stood around to stare that I could not see anything over their heads. I tried to work from a little elevated place, but they crowded all the more. They did not seem interested in my sketch, but apparently just liked to look at me, and enjoyed loafing there, doing nothing else by the hour, so that in the end all I could do was to draw them instead of the synagogue. They were perfectly good-natured about it, and seemed willing that I should make all the drawings of them I wanted.

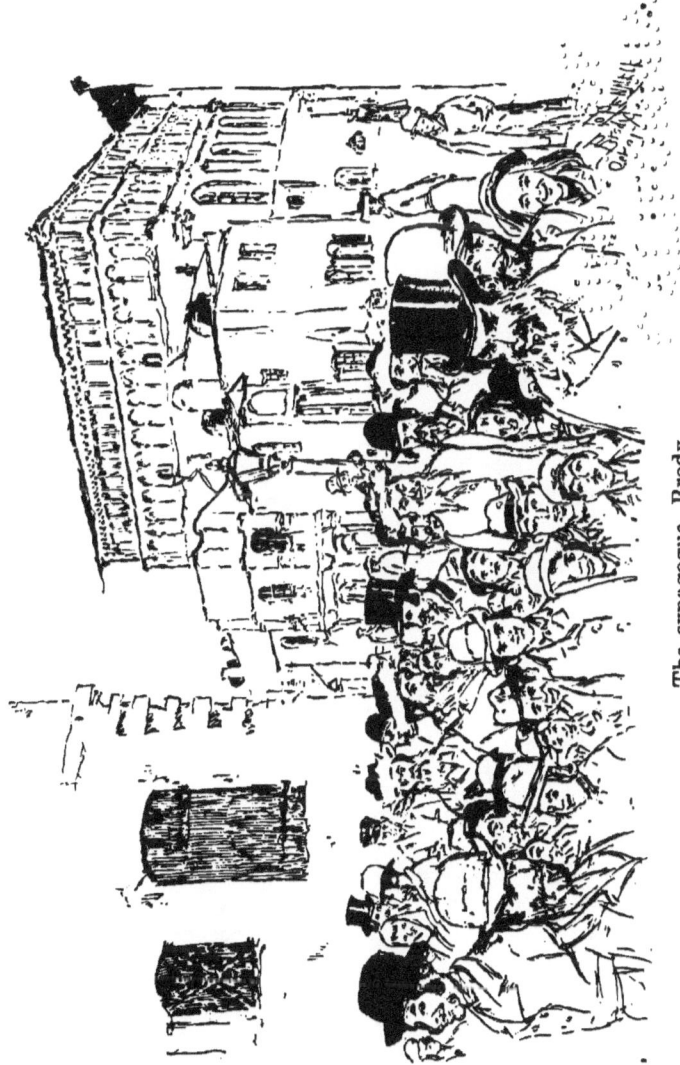

The synagogue, Brody.

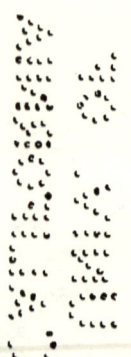

But, for all their amiability, I was always unpleasantly conscious that here were people who, despite their poverty, never work with their hands; whose town, except for its solitary Russian church, its sham classic castle, and the old plaques and brass lamps in the synagogue, contains nothing of beauty, and is but a hideous nightmare of dirt, disease, and poverty; and that all this misery and ugliness is in a large measure the outcome of their own habits and way of life, and not, as is usually supposed, forced upon them by Christian persecutors.

III.

IN RUSSIA.

FROM Brody I went to Kieff, and the minute I crossed the Russian frontier I encountered the Russian Jew. He is only the same Polish Jew, who here, instead of being an Austrian, is a Russian subject. But he is altogether different in costume and in many other respects. His ringlets are gone, and so are his top-hat and furry turban. He still keeps his hands buried in his sleeves, whether hanging at his side or crossed on his stomach, and the caftan still remains, though it is in no way remarkable in Russia, where everybody, in winter at least, has on a coat down to his heels. He looks about as miserable as in Austria, from

The Russian Jew.

the same causes I have noted; but he is not so conspicuous, since he wears the same big cap, drawn down to his ears, and the same high boots and gum shoes as the Russian. To say that in this part of Russia he looks more wretched than the Jew across the border is to confess that one knows little about him.

It was on my way to Kieff that I was afforded—I am afraid not knowingly—by the Russian Government an example of how they really do treat him. It is only necessary to see a Russian eviction once to make you for the time being throw aside all your reason for sentiment. The train I was in drew up at about two in the morning, and stopped there for its usual half-hour. It was so dark where I was, for the train was enormously long and my car near the head of it, that I could not make out the name of the place. The three bells were rung, and the other complicated signals gone through, and then I suddenly noticed that the engine, and not the train, went off. At the same time I heard just under my window a scuffling and some women crying. I thought it might be worth while to look out. I went to the door of the car. On the platform, right in front of me, I could just see a huddled-up group of people a few yards ahead. I walked toward them; there were two old Jews, a couple of younger men, two or three women, and some children. They were accompanied by four soldiers, in little black caps and huge overcoats, with immense swords, which they held drawn in their hands. There was a sergeant or corporal with them. The engine and the luggage van came slowly back, having picked up a car which, as there was a light inside, I could see had grated windows. It stopped; two of the Cossacks—one knows what a Cossack is a few hours after one has been in this part of Russia— seized one of the oldest Jews, who was literally doubled up under a great bag, and shoved him toward the car. He stumbled, and a few miserable old rags, some tin pots, and broken bread rolled on the platform and on the track, but he was half thrown, half dragged, out of sight; the rest were pushed in after him as roughly as a man who had only one hand to use, while he

In the park, Brody.

held his sword in the other, could do it; a porter was called by the sergeant to pick up

what he could find in a minute or two of the
old Jew's possessions, and the train moved off.
A couple of the Cossacks were laughing on the
platform, the porters said not a word, and there
was not another man about to see this, I suppose, trivial example of Russian authority. The
putting of half a dozen people into the train
by sufficient force to have moved ten times
their number was the worst instance of child-
ishness and brutality that I have ever witnessed.
Where the Jews went I do not know. When
I again awoke, in the morning, and looked out
the van had disappeared, and about ten o'clock
I got to Kieff.

Kieff is chiefly notable, so far as the Jews
go, for its un-Jewish character. For while the
Jews monopolize some of the few trades of the
town which they are still allowed to pursue,
they do not monopolize one's attention, as in
almost all the other places to which I went.
Nothing could be more absurd than the action
of the Kieff authorities in turning out all the

The market at Kieff.

Jew musicians from the theatres; still more serious was their prohibiting all Jews from being carters and cooks. And yet, although these steps have been taken recently, not only do you now find the entire fur and clothing business in their hands, not only do you see them in the markets in the lower parts of the town selling the cheapest and worst possible stuffs and sham goods to the peasants at the highest possible prices, but they seem as perfectly happy and contented as in Austria, showing no dread of future expulsion or loss of present business.

It is quite true that they can only live in two quarters of the town (and even there, it is said, only on suffrage), one of which has been appropriated by the richer class of Jews, the other by the poorer; but certainly none of them, rich or poor, in their shops or in their houses, look as if they thought their life in Russia was hanging by a single thread. As I saw the Polish Jew in Kieff, in Berdicheff, and on the Russian frontier, he was no poorer, no

10

more miserable, no dirtier, no more a subject of deserving pity than the Polish Jew in Austria or Hungary. To compare Kieff with an Austrian town like Lemberg is to learn how slight is the difference in their condition in the country where they are free men. If in Kieff the poorer Jews are compelled to live in a certain part of the town, in Lemberg they do so now from choice. In both their quarters are near the great city markets, in both they are dealers in all sorts of small wares for the peasants, in both they have a monopoly in old clothes, and in both they are forever squabbling, bargaining, haggling together and with the peasants. In some respects they are better off in Russia. For the poorer Jewish quarter of Kieff is comparatively clean, the sanitary regulations are strictly enforced, and the streets as well attended to as in any other part of the town. In Lemberg, though the rest of the city was marvelously clean, and though it was snowing when I got there, the streets were being swept

Lemberg.

everywhere except in the filthy Jewish quarter. Lemberg contains street after street of im-
posing new apartment houses, with shops on
the ground floor, very pretentious, like all of
Austria-Hungary; those in which the natives
live are clean, but those taken possession of by
the Jews are unspeakably dirty, dirtier than
anything I saw in Russia. It might be thought
from this that the authorities of Lemberg did
not care what became of the Jews, were not
the same dirt and filth found in the Jewish
quarter of every Austrian town.

Much sentiment has been wasted over the
poverty-stricken appearance of the Russian Jew,
his consumptive, hollow-chested look, and his
shambling walk. But if the most cheerful and
best-fed man in Europe will turn up his coat-
collar at the back, cross his hands on the pit
of his stomach, and bury them in his sleeves,
look out of the corners of his eyes and well
project his under lip, he could make himself
into the most beautiful example of a distressed

Russian Jew you could want; even an Adonis
or a Hercules would be at once reduced to an
object of pity and charity.

The Jew naturally is not physically weaker
than the peasant. As a soldier, when he is
made to stand up straight, he is as fine a man
as any other Russian, with the exception that
he can not march as well, but becomes quickly
footsore. This is because he never takes any
exercise; he never walks, he never carries any
burdens—in fact, he never uses his hands or his
legs if he can help it. In Hungary, when the
Jew is too poor or unable to get a peasant to
drive him in his cart, he can still load a gypsy
with all his traps, or, as a last resource, his wife
becomes his beast of burden. If his hair and
beard were decently cut and trimmed, the look
of ill-health would quickly disappear from his
face. The real wonder is that the filth with
which he surrounds himself does not undermine
his constitution forever. That he lives long
enough is proved by the large number of old

A street, Berdichell.

gray-headed Polish Jews one sees in every Jewish town.

The hatred which the Russians and everybody else you meet in Kieff have for the Jew is intense. They even go so far in their prejudice as to tell you that his being forcibly—often cruelly—expelled is his own fault; that when he is told to go, he refuses to get his passport or sell his goods; that, consequently, when he is actually turned out, he has no passport, no money, and can not go. The Government, therefore, sends him to the frontier; but when he arrives there and can not cross it without the necessary passport, he is probably dispatched to prison, where he stays until they are tired of keeping him. As far as I can see, the only difference in this matter between a Jew and a Christian is that the Christian would make a still stronger resistance, a harder fight for his rights. Nevertheless, it is on such arguments that the Russians base the defense of their treatment of the Jews. On the other hand, no one

11

who has seen the Jew in Russia can wonder that they want to get rid of a creature who is so clannish and so dirty, who is so entirely bent on making a little money for himself, whose shops in the large and commercial towns are always the meanest—in a word, whose every action is calculated to foster and keep alive that hatred or race - prejudice which has existed against him ever since he first turned up in Egypt. He has schools for his children in these Russian towns; but apparently it is chiefly that they may learn Hebrew, a language which the rest of the people can not understand, the knowledge of which marks them more than ever as a race apart.

Little as I saw of Russia, I was fortunate enough to go to both a great Jewish and a great Christian center. To Kieff the peasant pilgrims come to-day, inspired by a religious fervor which I do not believe was ever surpassed in the middle ages, while the barbaric splendor and magnificence of the churches would impress the least impressionable. Berdicheff, too, is a great pilgrimage place for the Jew. There the pilgrims crowd, not from any love of religion,

Bargaining in the bazaar, Berdicheff.

but eager to barter and to buy. Kieff is filled with beauty, Berdicheff with misery. In this great city of one hundred thousand people, nine-

ty thousand of whom are Jews, there are only
two buildings which are worthy of the least
attention—the Roman Catholic and the Russian
churches. The rest of the town is completely
given over to the great bazaars in which the
big fairs are held. The churches even struggle
with the Jewish shops, which have burrowed
underneath them and have been carried up to
the very doors. Among almost every people,
except these Jews, the business man has a pride
in his shop, a pride which, though it may only
express itself in an attempt to be more gaudy
and pretentious than his rival or his neighbor, is
at least healthy. But the Jew is without all
such feeling. In a huge trading center like
Berdicheff, where the largest Jewish fair in the
world, I believe, is held, a cellar, a garret, or a
shed is quite good enough for the Jew merchant
or dealer. Nor can it be argued that he does
not build shops because he is afraid of being
turned out, since he manages his business in
exactly the same way wherever he goes — in

Brody and Márámaros Sziget as in Berdicheff. He shows an absolute unwillingness to do anything to benefit the town to which he belongs or the people among whom he lives. In the country he is much the same as in the town. If

A café scene.—A contrast of types.

the Hungarian does not want him to have land, it is because the Jew's only object in getting it is not to make it his own, not to improve it, but to farm it out, to play the middleman. He does not work it himself, and this is opposed to all Hungarian ideas, to the very principles for which they fought in the great revolution of '48.

The Polish Jew to-day may be what centuries of persecution and oppression have made him. Christians may really be responsible for the characteristics which render him most repulsive in Christian eyes; a fact to be regretted, just as the degeneration of any race by force of circumstances—by change of climate or geological conditions—is to be deplored. But the work of long years can not be undone in a day, and to civilize the Polish Jew according to our standard is about as difficult a task as to civilize the red Indian. Habits of old thrust upon him have at last become instinctive. In Russia and Austria-Hungary he has outgrown the character supposed to be typically Jewish. He may be a trifle keener and cleverer than the Russian peas-

In the streets of Brody.

ant, who is, perhaps, the dullest creature God ever made; but that is the whole extent of his cleverness. A poor Jew in the West was once thought a physical and moral impossibility; in a country like mediæval England, despite persecution more relentless and cruel than that to which he is now subjected in Russia, he throve and prospered and was always rich. The average Polish Jew in Russia not only is wretchedly poor, but he seems reconciled to his poverty. What the personal morals of the Jew, whose chastity is his great boast, may be in these countries, I have no means of judging; but I know that if he thinks he can increase his own gains by pandering to the immorality of others, he is quite ready to do so. In small Austrian towns of five or six hundred inhabitants I have had overtures made to me by Jews in curls and caftan which hitherto I had never heard even suggested, save in the large cities of western Europe. Nor is he in other ways more virtuous and orderly than his Christian fellow-

12

citizen, much as his superior virtue is vaunted.
I have already referred to the statement of the
authorities of Márámaros Sziget, that by far the
greater number of thieves in their prisons were
Jews. In Vienna, the only place where I found
a special policeman on duty—except, of course,
the mounted police, who direct the traffic in the
larger thoroughfares—was in front of a drink-
ing-house, used as an old-clothes exchange, in
the Judengasse, and he scarcely would have
been there without good reason.

It should also be remembered by those who
are spending their sentiment and cash on the
Russian Jews that in a large part of Little Russia they are not Jews at all—that is, by race—
but descendants not of Semites from Judea, but
of that Tartar tribe who were converted to
Judaism centuries ago, at the time when it
seemed likely that the whole of southern Russia would become a Jewish empire. And a great
pity it did not, for then the Russian Jews would
have kept to their own home, and not come

wandering westward to add to the already over-
numerous social and industrial problems of England and America.

As he comes westward, the Jew does not

Type of Sziget Jew.

put off his Russian ways with the Russian yoke.
It is because he remains practically the same—

his peculiarities exaggerated rather than toned down—when he settles himself in Austria and Hungary, that it is so much more instructive just now to study him in those countries than in Russia. It is but the occasional Russian Jew who pushes himself to the front and makes his way to and in the Hungarian capital; for, though Buda - Pesth is, fast becoming a great Jewish town, the majority of its rich Jews are Germans or Hungarians. The Russian or Polish Jew there, as a rule, is as greasy and dirty and poor as in Berdicheff. When he does so ex-ceptionally rise in the Hungarian world, this is the manner of his rising, as Hungarians explain it: In the first generation he comes to Márá-maros Sziget, or some other town near the front-ier; in the second, he keeps an inn in the mount-ains of Márámaros or Transylvania, or, better still, in the great Hungarian plain; in the third, he reaches Buda-Pesth; in the fourth, he makes his fortune; in the fifth, he spends it, and goes back to begin all over again; and it must be

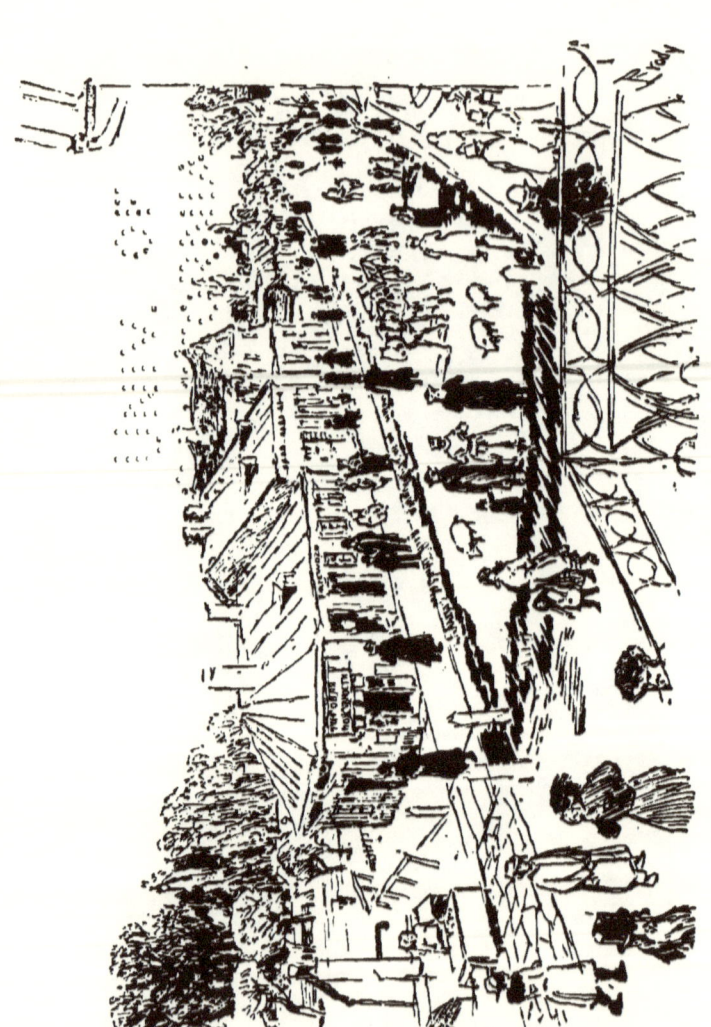

Brody.—The street is nothing more than an open sewer.

borne in mind that it is not the fifth—of whom something might be made—but the first, with whom we have to deal under Baron Hirsch's great scheme. The majority remain as I have described them in Sziget and Brody, indifferent to all the decencies of life, reviving the grotesque curls of which they are shorn in Russia, and relapsing into the dirt in which—and perhaps this is one of their chief grievances against the Russian Government—they are not so free to wallow in Russia. Unpleasant as is Berdicheff, it is beautifully clean compared to the Jewish quarters of Sziget and Brody. With their liberty they sink deeper into, instead of seeking to escape from, the degradation which we are charitable enough to think entirely the result of Russian persecution. They like dirt; they like to herd together in human pigsties; they like to live on worse than nothing — on food which would not be enough even for the abstemious Slovak; they like to make money out of the immorality of the Christian. They

are simply a race of middlemen and money-
changers. Is it any wonder, then, that in Austria-Hungary the people feel about them very
much as the Americans felt about the China-
men? Nor does the Polish Jew do better when
he moves or is moved still farther westward.
Ask the Whitechapel workman what he thinks
of the Polish Jew, who, because he can exist
on a miserable wage, threatens to supplant the
native. Or ask the New Yorker who has to
come in contact with him in the struggle for
bread and butter his opinion of the thirty-five
thousand now living in and about the Bowery.

To see the Polish Jew at home is to understand the desire of Continental philanthropists
to establish him in colonies over the sea. To
get rid of him is the sole object of Russians, to
keep him out of their country the chief end of
Austrians and Hungarians. Jews of other na-
tionalities themselves are as eager to be done
with him forever. Millionaires of Hamburg
give their thousands cheerfully to encourage a

Type of Polish Jew.

13

new exodus which will prevent his settling in
Germany and perhaps injuring the millionaires'
business; what he does in England and America is of no importance to the gentlemen of
Hamburg. Scattered here and there, singly and
alone, the Polish Jew might become as desira-
ble a citizen as any one else. Brought away in
families and colonies, as the Austrian or Hungarian knows, he is as serious a demoralizing
factor in the community as the Chinaman, and
to be kept out at any cost. Even the Turk,
himself not an overclean animal, knows this,
and refuses to receive Jewish families into the
Ottoman Empire, basing his refusal on sanitary
grounds. Probably Austrians and Hungarians
will hold their peace until the present emigra-
tion fever is over, for the more who are trans-
ported to lands far from Russia the fewer will
be left to come crowding across the frontier
into Austria-Hungary.

Any one who has traveled the main Russian
railway from the great junction where the lines

from St. Petersburg, Moscow, Kieff, and Odessa
come together, down to Woloczyska, knows why
the Austrian fears the Jew. Into the towns
which lie near this line for years the Russians
have been pushing the Jews. Every town over-
flows with them. As you pass in the train you
see their long black figures stalking across the
fields, and as your carriage comes to a stop you
imagine you have arrived in a new Jerusalem.
The merest wayside station is crowded with
them; they block up the exits and the en-
trances; comparatively few get on or off the
train, though these Jews will travel any dis-
tance if by doing so they can handle enough
money to cover their railway ticket. The ex-
cuse which permits them to overrun the Russian railway stations is that they have come for
their letters. But while you may see one or
two get a postcard, fifty or a hundred are simply standing there waiting for something to turn
up. If the Russians have been able to concen-
trate such a large proportion of their Jewish

population right on the Austrian frontier, the
Austrians, who know both the Russians and the
Jews, will ask you what there is to prevent
the former from some day dumping these poor,
wretched, useless people right into their coun-

On the frontier.

try? It is this dread which has been the greatest ally of Baron Hirsch in his own land. To
say that the Russians would be afraid of the
consequences is not to know anything about
the country or the people. It is this dread

which is enabling Baron Hirsch to buy land in the Argentine Republic at four times its value, and to transplant thither his brethren, of whom he is so terribly anxious to be rid. But, according to the latest advices from South America, they have no intention of causing the desert to blossom as the rose, and they are leaving their farms and their stock and are making for the more promising pastures in the heart of the South American cities.

That the Polish Jews are only too ready to accept the money given them and to journey to far countries can be explained without referring to the tyranny from which they are supposed to long to escape. Peasants at home in a land and attached to the soil would often be as ready. The poor Jew thinks, as so many other and better men have thought before him, that once in America or England his fortune is made; and he arrives there usually only to be sweated as he was at home, only to live as miserably and wretchedly. He is no better off,

In South America.

while the people into whose midst he is brought
are far worse off. There is no more pathetic
figure in history than this poor wretch whom
nobody wants, who is an outcast wherever he
goes. When we see him at a respectful dis-
tance, all our sympathies are stirred and we
welcome any movement in his behalf. But the
better we know him the more anxious we are
that some one else, not ourselves, should be
chosen to solve his problem.

THE END.

.

14

*T*HE SOVEREIGNS AND COURTS OF EUROPE. The Home and Court Life and Characteristics of the Reigning Families. By "POLITIKOS." With many Portraits. 12mo. Cloth, $1.50.

"A remarkably able book. . . . A great deal of the inner history of Europe is to be found in the work, and it is illustrated by admirable portraits."—*The Athenæum.*

"Its chief merit is that it gives a new view of several sovereigns. . . . The anonymous author seems to have sources of information that are not open to the foreign correspondents who generally try to convey the impression that they are on terms of intimacy with royalty."—*San Francisco Chronicle.*

"A most entertaining volume, which is evidently the work of a singularly well-informed writer. The vivid descriptions of the home and court life of the various royalties convey exactly the knowledge of character and the means of a personal estimate which will be valued by intelligent readers."—*Toronto Mail.*

"The anonymous author of these sketches of the reigning sovereigns of Europe appears to have gathered a good deal of curious information about their private lives, manners, and customs, and has certainly in several instances had access to unusual sources. The result is a volume which furnishes views of the kings and queens concerned, far fuller and more intimate than can be found elsewhere."—*New York Tribune.*

" . . A book that would give the truth, the whole truth, and nothing but the truth (so far as such comprehensive accuracy is possible), about these exalted personages, so often heard about but so seldom seen by ordinary mortals, was a desideratum, and this book seems well fitted to satisfy the demand. The author is a well-known writer on questions indicated by his pseudonym."—*Montreal Gazette.*

"A very handy book of reference. '—*Boston Transcript.*

*M*Y CANADIAN JOURNAL, 1872-'78. By LADY DUFFERIN, author of "Our Vice-Regal Life in India." Extracts from letters home written while Lord Dufferin was Governor-General of Canada. With Portrait, Map, and Illustrations from sketches by Lord Dufferin. 12mo. Cloth, $2.00.

"A graphic and intensely interesting portraiture of out-door life in the Dominion, and will become, we are confident, one of the standard works on the Dominion. . . . It is a charming volume."—*Boston Traveller.*

"In every place and under every condition of circumstances the Marchioness shows herself to be a true lady, without reference to her title. Her book is most entertaining, and the abounding good-humor of every page must stir a sympathetic spirit in its readers."—*Philadelphia Bulletin.*

"A very pleasantly written record of social functions in which the author was the leading figure; and many distinguished persons, Americans as well as Canadians, pass across the gayly decorated stage. The author is a careful observer, and jots down her impressions of people and their ways with a frankness that is at once entertaining and amusing."—*Book-Buyer.*

"The many readers of Lady Dufferin's Journal of "Our Vice-Regal Life in India" will welcome this similar record from the same vivacious pen, although it concerns a period antecedent to the other, and takes one back many years. The book consists of extracts from letters written home by Lady Dufferin to her friends (her mother chiefly), while her husband was Governor-General of Canada; and describes her experiences in the same chatty and charming style with which readers were before made familiar."—*Cincinnati Commercial-Gazette.*

*N*EW *FRAGMENTS.* By JOHN TYNDALL, F. R. S., author of " Fragments of Science," " Heat as a Mode of Motion," etc. 12mo. 500 pages. Cloth, $2.00.

Among the subjects treated in this volume are " The Sabbath," " Life in the Alps," " The Rainbow and its Congeners," " Common Water," and " Atoms, Molecules, and Ether-Waves." In addition to the popular treatment of scientific themes, the author devotes several chapters to biographical sketches of the utmost interest, including studies of Count Rumford and Thomas Young, and chapters on " Louis Pasteur, his Life and Labors," and " Personal Recollections of Thomas Carlyle."

" Tyndall is the happiest combination of the lover of nature and the lover of science, and these fragments are admirable examples of his delightful style, and proofs of his comprehensive intellect "—*Philadelphia Evening Bulletin.*

" The name of this illustrious scientist and *littérateur* is known wherever the English language is the mother tongue, or is even freely spoken. Whatever he does or says comes with a stamp of authority as from one who speaks with power, knowing whereof he affirms. He is able and effective. both as a talker and writer, as scientist or teacher. To those who know anything of Prof. Tyndall's life and labors, scientific or literary, it is superfluous to say that his utterances bring his hearers or readers face to face with the latest knowledge on the subject he discusses."—*New York Commercial Advertiser.*

*M*ORAL *TEACHINGS OF SCIENCE.* By ARABELLA B. BUCKLEY, author of " The Fairy-Land of Science," " Life and her Children," etc. 12mo. Cloth, 75 cents.

" The book is intended for readers who would not take up an elaborate philosophical work—those who, feeling puzzled and adrift in the present chaos of opinion, may welcome even a partial solution, from a scientific point of view, of the difficulties which oppress their minds."—*From the Preface.*

*M*AX *MÜLLER AND THE SCIENCE OF LANGUAGE.* A Criticism. By WILLIAM DWIGHT WHITNEY, Professor in Yale University. 12mo. 79 pages. Paper cover, 50 cents.

This critique relates to the new edition of Prof. Müller's well-known work on Language. " For many," says Prof. Whitney, in his preface, " the book has been their first introduction to linguistic study ; and doubtless to a large proportion of English-speaking readers, especially, it is still the principal and most authoritative text-book of that study, as regards both methods and results. A work holding such a position calls for careful criticism, that it may not be trusted where it is untrustworthy, and so do harm to the science which it was intended to help."

" This caustic review of Max Müller's latest edition of his ' Science of Language' will command attention for more and higher merits than its brilliant criticism. It upholds a theory of language and of its development which, though not taught by Max Müller, is held by the great masters of linguistic science. The reader not versed in the science, nor well read in its controversial literature, will get from this *brochure* a conception of the critical points of the subject which he might miss in the reading of many larger and more systematic treatises."—*The Independent,* New York.

A NEW BOOK BY THE AUTHOR OF "UNCLE REMUS."

BRER RABBIT PREACHES.

ON THE PLANTA-TION. By JOEL CHANDLER HARRIS. With numerous Illustrations by E. W. KEMBLE. 12mo. Cloth, $1.50.

The announcement of a new volume by Joel Chandler Harris will be welcomed by the host of readers who have found unlimited entertainment in the chronicles of *Uncle Remus*. *On the Plantation* abounds in stirring incidents, and in it the author presents a graphic picture of certain phases of Southern life which have not appeared in his books before. There are also some new examples of the folk-lore of the negroes which became classic when presented to the public in the pages of *Uncle Remus*.

This charming book has been elaborately illustrated by Mr. E. W. Kemble, whose thorough familiarity with Southern types is well known to the reading public. The book is uniform with *Uncle Remus*, and contains in all twenty-three illustrations.

From the Introductory Note.

" Some of my friends who have read in serial form the chronicles that follow profess to find in them something more than an autobiographical touch. Be it so. It would indeed be difficult to invest the commonplace character and adventures of Joe Maxwell with the vitality that belongs to fiction. Nevertheless, the lad himself, and the events which are herein described, seem to have been born of a dream. That which is fiction pure and simple in these pages bears to me the stamp of truth, and that which is true reads like a clumsy invention. In this matter it is not for me to prompt the reader. He must sift the fact from the fiction and label it to suit himself."

New York: D. APPLETON & CO., 1, 3, & 5 Bond Street.

THE LAST WORDS OF THOMAS CARLYLE.

Including *Wotton Reinfred*, Carlyle's only essay in fiction ; the *Excursion (Futile Enough) to Paris ;* and letters from Thomas Carlyle, also letters from Mrs. Carlyle, to a personal friend. With Portrait. 12mo. Cloth.

FROM THE INTRODUCTION.

"The two manuscripts included in 'The Last Words of Thomas Carlyle' were left among the author's papers at his death. One of them, 'Wotton Reinfred,' is Carlyle's only essay in fiction, and it therefore possesses so distinctive an interest that its omission from Carlyle's complete works would not be justifiable. The other, 'Excursion (Futile Enough) to Paris,' offers a vivid picture of Carlyle's personality. By the publication of these two manuscripts, with the accompanying letters, a new and considerable volume is added to the list of Carlyle's works.

"'Wotton Reinfred' was probably written soon after Carlyle's marriage, at the time when he and his wife entertained the idea of producing a novel in collaboration. The romance may be said to possess a peculiar psychological interest, inasmuch as it represents the earlier period of Carlyle's literary development. In the labored but not faulty style, the most familiar characteristics of the writer's later work are only occasionally apparent. So far as matter is concerned, the reader will not be slow to discover, in the conversations of Wotton and the Doctor, the first expression of ideas and doctrines afterward set forth with more formality in 'Sartor Resartus.' 'It is a poor philosophy which can be taught in words,' is the Doctor's proposition. 'We talk and talk, and talking without acting, though Socrates were the speaker, does not help our case, but aggravates it. Thou must act, thou must work, thou must do! Collect thyself, compose thyself, find what is wanting that so tortures thee, do but attempt with all thy strength to attain it, and thou art saved.' Here is the doctrine afterward expanded by Teufelsdröckh in 'Sartor Resartus.'

"Concerning Carlyle's judgment of his contemporaries he has often enlightened us with his wonted frankness, but in 'Wotton Reinfred' alone he appears as the writer of a romance whose characters are drawn from real life. On this point we may quote Mr. James Anthony Froude, who says :

"'The interest of "Wotton Reinfred" to me is considerable from the sketches which it contains of particular men and women, most of whom I knew and could, if necessary, identify. The story, too, is taking enerally from real life. and perhaps Carlyle did not finish it from the sense that it could not be published while the persons and things could be recognized. That objection to the publication no longer exists. Everybody is dead whose likenesses have been drawn, and the incidents stated have long been forgotten.'

"The 'Excursion (Futile Enough) to Paris' is the unreserved daily record of a journey in company with the Brownings, when Carlyle paid a visit to Lord Ashburton. That this record is characteristic, and that it presents a singularly vivid picture of the writer's personality, is self-evident. It is a picture which adds something to our knowledge of Carlyle the man, and is therefore worth preservation. The world has long since known that even Carlyle's heroic figure may claim the sympathy and pity due a great soul fretting against its material environments."

New York : D. APPLETON & CO., 1, 3, & 5 Bond Street.

www.ingramcontent.com/pod-product-compliance
Lightning Source LLC
Chambersburg PA
CBHW022341020726
47500CB00004B/1228